BARN DANCE!

By Bill Martin Jr.
and John Archambault

Illustrated by Ted Rand

SCHOLASTIC INC.
New York Toronto London Auckland Sydney
Mexico City New Delhi Hong Kong

Full moon shinin', shinin' big an' bright,
Pushin' back the shadows, holdin' back the night.
Not a thing stirrin', quiet as could be,
Just the whisper of the leaves on the cottonwood tree.

Ol' houn' dog, whinin' in his sleep,
Dreamin' after rabbits in a game of hide 'n seek.
Over in the farmhouse, all the lights were out,
Farmer an' his wife an' kids, not a one about—

All except the skinny kid with questions in his head,
Much too full of wonderment to spend the night in bed,
He was up about an' list'nin'. . .

. . . when the night owl said,
Come a little closer . . .
Come a little closer . . .
Listen to the night . . .
There's magic in the air . . . .

Then the skinny kid heard it . . . heard it faint begin . . .
A *plink! plink! plink!* on the wind's violin . . .
Comin' from the corn field . . . sweet 'n soft 'n low . . .
Music honeyed up by the ol' scarecrow . . .
A-plinkin' on the fiddle strings to tune 'em up just so . . . .

The scarecrow tucked the fiddle underneath his chin
An' fiddled out a welcome to all his country kin.
He fiddled through the woods 'n fields 'n all aroun' the farm,
Biddin' ever'body come to a hoedown in the barn.

There was so much chit 'n chatter when the critters all arrived,
That no one saw the skinny kid oozle in an' hide
Just in time to hear the crow call the dance, *Begin!*
Grab yourself a partner an' jump right in!

Right hand! Left hand! Around you go!
Now back-to-back your partner in a do-si-do!
Mules to the center for a curtsey an' a bow!
An' hey there, skinny kid! Show the old cow how!

Out came the skinny kid, a-tickin' an' a-tockin'
An' a hummin' an' a-yeein' an' a-rockin' an' a-sockin'.
An' he danced his little toe through a hole in his stockin'!

He leaped the apple barrel an' the pun'kins in a pile,
An' he showed 'em how to wagon-wheel, barnyard style.
Now rocket to the moon an' powder-puff your noses,
An' hurry home to mama on your little pink toeses!

Five times! Ten times! Fifteen! Twenty!
Now spin once again an' that's a-plenty!
But the fat little pigs whirled 'round 'n 'round,
'Till they got so dizzy that they all fell down.

The sky was warmin' up for the comin' of the day
When the skinny kid . . . heard . . . the night owl . . . say,

Mornin's comin' closer . . .
Mornin's comin' closer . . .
The magic time is over . . .
Night'll soon be gone . . . .

The ol' dog stretched 'n blinked a sleepy eye
Just a blink too late to see the skinny kid slip by . . .

He tiptoed through the kitchen . . . an' tiptoed up the stairs . . .
As quiet as a feather . . . on a breath of air . . . .

He hummed a little do-si-do an' flopped himself in bed . . .
With the wonders of the barn dance . . . dancin' in his head.

For my father, Virgil Archambault,
first of Terrebonne, Minnesota,
and now of Sierra Madre, California,
a born barn dancer in step and spirit.

John Archambault

ISBN 0-439-22847-6

Text copyright © 1986 by Bill Martin Jr. and John Archambault.
Illustrations copyright © 1986 by Ted Rand.
All rights reserved. Published by Scholastic Inc.,
555 Broadway, New York, NY 10012,
by arrangement with Henry Holt and Company, Inc.
SCHOLASTIC and associated logos are trademarks
and/or registered trademarks of Scholastic Inc.

12 11 10 9 8 7 6   4 5/0

Printed in the U.S.A.   08

In an old farmhouse, bathed in the light of a full moon, a young boy creeps to his bedroom window and looks outside. Was that a voice he just heard, or the hooting of an owl? There it is again:

> *Come a little closer . . .*
> *Come a little closer . . .*
> *Listen to the night . . .*
> *There's magic in the air. . . .*

Beckoned by the voice, the boy sneaks downstairs, out the door, and walks toward the barn. As he gets closer he hears the sweet sound of a country fiddler and the rhythmic thumping of dancing feet. But who could possibly be having a barn dance in the middle of the night?

"Sheer magic! A fun-filled romp ideal for reading aloud." —*Childhood Education*

★ "A rousing, rowdy tale pulsing with the rhythm of country music. . . . Rand's raucous . . . watercolor spreads are as spirited as the story poem." —*Booklist* (starred review)

★ "An engaging blend of words and pictures to set both the mind and eye dancing."
—*Scbool Library Journal* (starred review)

This edition is only available for distribution through the school market.

SCHOLASTIC INC.

0-439-22847-6